The Color of Beauty

The Color of Beauty

Dex Hopes

Published by DEX HOPES, 2024.

This is a work of fiction. Similarities to real people, places, or events are entirely coincidental.

THE COLOR OF BEAUTY

First edition. June 13, 2024.

Copyright © 2024 Dex Hopes.

ISBN: 979-8224560141

Written by Dex Hopes.

I would like to dedicate this book to my wonderful parents

Mr .& Mrs. Tom Hopes

also

Reneece Lenae & Dex II

Hello all, I go by or should I say write under the name "Flex"

I would not consider myself a Poet or maybe not even a Writer, I'm a person who just likes to express life the way I've experienced and viewed.

I speak deep from within. Some of the pieces might have you either

Laughing, Emotional or just feeling Proud.

My inspiration comes from family friends and you, the very unique people who walk the streets and say hello. Thank you all....

My Life

Many times throughout life I was saddened by the color of
my skin
Trying my best to fit in if not just blend in
Always embarrassed by the redness of my eyes
Never looking face to face and
pretending to be shy
Talking very fast as if it was a foreign language
Taking my time and slowing it down was something I never
could manage
Wondering if I could ever be normal or like everyone else
All I ever wanted was to be loved and
not left by myself
All these emotions I had were so hard to shake
Well, up until the day I found my Soulmate

Thank You Mom & Dad

I want to first thank God for giving me the courage to pursue my passion of expression, the ability to reach out and welcome in so
much that life has to offer.
I want to thank my wonderful parents Mr. Tom & Mrs. Willie B Hopes, the best mom and pops I could ever have. You gave me the drive, strength and determination to keep pushing through whatever my heart is feeling. The constant reminder that reading is so important. The everyday reminder that being polite to others is a must, always respect the people you come in contact with, because you never know what they're dealing with. You both allowed me to be free with my writing even if it was edgy, just speak your heart and use correct grammar. I'm not at this point, if you both don't show me what love and family are all about. Thank you both for showing me there is so much goodness in life and in people. Mom, like you always said, "Don't worry if people don't like you, some people didn't like Jesus Christ". Because of those words, it's given me the strength to keep on loving no matter the situation.

THANK YOU

Thank You D & Ren

Thank you D & Ren, what more can I say to even begin to say thank you
for the growth you both sent my way.
Just a young pop trying to do right and sometimes I wasn't always correct but you
both loved me anyway. I brag about the "Joy of Fatherhood" because nothing
touches.
my heart more than to be your Dad.
D, you stayed close as my sidekick not even having a best friend, you had teammates
but not a true play mate. Wherever I rolled you rolled, hanging with pops and his
boys. That would explain your older Soul.
Growing up having our heart to hearts, talking life, women, music and more life.
Watching you do your thing on the court and on the field,
I wasn't a parent at those moments I became a fan.
A proud Dad I was watching the growth of you become a solid man.
There weren't many moments when our boys would ask "Where's the other Dex"
Back when we both balled at the same time, you telling me "Dad I got you go deep,
or me yelling "Pull up D your open for the three" Those became The Reason for
Writing
Thanks for holding it down for me during my weakest moments,
stepping in and making sure my head was straight.
D, you're not just my son, you are my Best Friend

Baby Ren, my first born my first chance at fatherhood. You sure turned out to be the strength of so many, never had to tell you much, you just always seemed to want to lead and be heard. I swear you're from a different time Throwback Queen. You knew early on that life wasn't fair to everyone; you learned to accept, stay the course teach those who had the courage to listen. The beautiful queen you always been, then turned that beauty on to your name sake Baby Girl aka Reneece Jr. Your journey from youth to adulthood has made you into something special. You never blamed anyone for whatever obstacles were in your path, you took it all as a learning experience. A true throwback queen you are,

going over our historic past that now your sons understand what it means to be

"Black & Proud"

You loved yourself because that's what we are left with, the beauty you see in the mirror.

Ren you have been my sidekick queen from McDonald's playland to seeing Obama make history.

You're such the perfect Mom, thanks for giving me the strength and the history lessons when sometimes I might forget. You're not only my sweet Baby Ren, your also my mentor.

Love you both dearly.

Dad

"The Middle Child"

Wow where can I begin.... You both have done so much for me in the lifetime of years you've known me. I'm not where I am as your little and big brother without you both. Always by my side whenever I needed anything, I never had to ask, you both just stepped in and made the situation better. From the help of raising my kids to making sure I'm always healthy, you both just appeared to make everything much better.

Never felt completely alone cause I always knew I had a big sister and little sister that would be there in less than five minutes. Being the only boy, I was protected and spoiled by you both. The security blanket never left Park Hill, it stayed attached for this lifetime. Losing Moms was such a blow, but I never felt I was without the nurturing Mom's provided, you both stepped in and displayed the love and care I needed.

I'm the middle child and I was always guarded from every direction. You both are so quick to say "that's my brother" I tried my best to live up to the pedestal you quietly placed me on. This moment, this happiness, this family love is not present without you Sharon and Tommie. Yes I'm the middle child but I couldn't have been more loved and safe than I am at this very moment cause I was covered by many directions .... Thank you from the bottom of my heart for a lifetime of love

Dex your brother....

"The Middle Child"

Chapter 1
Encouragement
"Its Beauty in the struggle
Ugliness in the success"
(J . Cole)

A mind never stops

A mind never stops, it's always going places.
Enjoy a journey not yet taken and stories of
those who are willing to share theirs.

Open up your Soul to pull in some Happiness.
Happiness isn't guaranteed, it's Created.
Let your heart be truthful.
That way your smile will last much longer.

Daddy's Little girl always

Happy Birthday Baby Ren

Your just the perfect Gift a Dad could ask for

God is so good, cause he Blessed me with you

Best Friend

Having a Best Friend is special and hard to come by
They're the ones by your side and
always hearing you cry
Having a Best Friend are the ones that hear your pain and
rage.
Having a Best Friend is the ones that make sure your always
safe.
Having a Best Friend is the one you tell your embarrassing
secrets.
They're the ones that keep it tight lipped.
and never leak it.
Having a Best Friend is the one you.
call your Ride or Die
Their holding your hand saying I love you.
till the final goodbye

Daddy's Girl

Stay focused on your dream.
You'll have awkward moments and days.
But your intellect will always prevail.
You're doing well. Don't get down or
discouraged.
Keep believing in your ability.
God will hold your hand and we all will
witness your success.
I promise.

Birthday card from a friend

Dex
It's your Birthday.
A day to celebrate you.
This is what I know about you Dex.
Your face is kind.
Your smile is sexy.
Your soul is beautiful.
You listen.
You encourage.
You challenge.
You understand.
You support.
You care.
You're deep.
You're thoughtful.
You're magnetic and energetic.
Your laughter is contagious.
Your essence is true and compassionate.
Your bring out the best in everyone you love
I treasure your friendship and all that YOU are.
Love Robin

Going to Class

My Joy is just to be a better person each day.
I wake up and go to class.
The classroom of life and learning from it
Sometimes we don't pay close attention, so we
skip a beat.
But there are times when we are fully focused.
Then it all makes sense

My Dad

In 1985 when most men were turning away from their children, you were there ready to be a Dad.

You were there showing me how a man and dad should be. Forever working hard and always letting me know you love me, you're much appreciated.

I'm thankful for your no weave, no fake nails, rules when I was a child. I grew up into a woman who loves herself (naturally) and I have a Dad who helped with that by always telling me I'm a beautiful black Beauty

I love you and am proud you're my Dad! Love you!!!
Happy Father's Day!

Hobbies to Live By

Life is what you make of it and also what you take from it.
Dreaming about something or somebody is a reality when it's met
with pursuit and persistence.
Happiness comes along when you take control of your own smile and
not being led away from your own energy.
Smiling I see as a contagious body function; you might catch it from
the very people who brighten your day.
Make it Happen.

Humbleness

It's great to be humble.
Being humble I believe brings more Blessings.
God sees your efforts of appreciation for
others.
Then places a wonderful pathway for you to
follow.
It's True

Mentor of life

Every morning there's always a hello, how are you?
My day hasn't quite begun until those words are mentioned.
You make sure every moment in the day that I take.
Is met with your words of care concern and best wishes.
Never do I have to wonder or ponder if you will be there.
Since day one when you became a part of my life you made it like a daily checklist
You never judge you just care, you never ask why, your just there.
My days aren't always the best of days, but always better after we talk.
I'm not the most well-polished this I know.
But every day you make me feel as if know one can outshine me.
There's always that "Good morning" but also that "Good Night."
My days have been so much better since you walked into my life.

Just friends

Your different than the norm, not like all the rest
Trying not to cross that line, trying not to press
Your my homegirl ...my dinner buddy... my best friend
You're the one I can call at all hours ....your there till the end
After a late night, you're not leaving.. not kicking you out
You can go upstairs sleep in my bed; I can crash here on the
couch.
Sometimes things are better when left alone.
Your my good friend, so I know I'll always have a home

Special Edition

Ain't no Nigga like me, I stand alone.
Not with arrogance but oddness
I have my own category.
My Mind Thoughts & Vison is what men envy and women crave.
Too Authentic ... a one-of-a-kind model.
Special Edition only 1 made in 1965, can't be duplicated.
Snatch it up, It's a Classic
Men hate to hear my voice .... Women are like "Tell me more"
It's a mindset made from a humbled past of many disappointments.
But was able to see a brighter future when he believed in himself and
happiness.
This man has fallen a many times but never broke
The love around him picked him up. Dusted him off and said
"Tomorrow is a New Day"

Life's Lessons

I would rather work hard to give the best of everything to someone I can afford.

Rather than bust my tail for someone who I can't afford and is in need of nothing.

One of life's lessons it took 20 years to figure out.

Friend

I have a beautiful friend, more like a brother to me. He's incredible, he
sees so much in me.
He listens and guides me, and shows me the light, because I'm not
always wise to this life.
He doesn't judge how I live, he simply encourages the love that I give.
I've never felt beautiful, or lovely and carefree. I've always just
been...me.
I am a woman with heart, full of love and forgiveness. It took him and
his words to help me see that I have so much to give.
I'll always be grateful, you see..I am free. He opened my eyes to see the
real me.
My brother... my Dex...I really don't know what to say next.
I thank you, I do. Simply, from me to you.
I love you I do... I'm so glad to know the real you!!!

Monica

On my sleeve

On my sleeve I wear it
The joy the pain
The laughter the shame
On my sleeve I put out positive vibes
So we all can laugh and giggle inside
On my sleeve I wear it
Crazy times and shit I'm going through.
My crew is deep, so I'm never alone it's more like "Us too."
On my sleeves I wear it
The happiest times placed before my eyes.
Maybe I'm being too honest, too afraid to lie.
On my sleeve I wear it
Never quiet.... always something to say.
Everyone's a witness, so I'm always on display.
On my sleeve is where its placed
So every day I wear it

Patience

Be patient God has already grabbed your hand.
Watch what he has in place for you.
Life is good but it's better when it's Amazing.
People and Circumstances are placed before us
for a reason.
It's up to us to figure out the purpose of both.

Powerful Words

1 Corinthians 13:11

31

When I was a child, I spoke as a child,
I understood as a child,
I thought as a child; but when I became a
man,
I put away childish things

Powerful Words

Proverbs 13:22:

A good man leaves an inheritance to his children's children, but the wealth of the sinner is stored up for the righteous. In God's book, a good man thinks generationally. He does not just prepare for his children's future, but for his grandchildren's.

She is

She shares her wisdom.
Always there to listen.
She's never one to judge.
She cares ..she loves
She's not the biggest thing walking.
But strong enough to lean on
She's brilliant enough to keep creating.
Humble enough to appreciate the Blessings.
She's a loyal friend, everyone adores her.
Looks like I raised her right.
She's a Queen

She's also my Daughter.

Simple Words

I just do lots of positive thinking. It keeps me
smiling and caring for others.
I just never understood arrogance or
mean-spirited people. Really no need for that.
Even through the hardest of times I continued
to believe in happiness.
If you give up on happiness, then you've
depleted the options of dreaming.
If you can dream anything is possible

Strictly For My Ni**a's

Right on Fella's for being there 30 & 40 plus years.
Dawg when I was hungry broke and shedding many Tears.
You didn't even know it then, but I have to keep it Real.
Starving when your calls were "swing through I'm firing up the Grill."
Being loud and cussing was something I never could Manage.
Even in your homes, it was never ... "Yo Dex watch your language."
I wasn't the perfect Dad and may have done things Wrong
Thanks for stepping in fella's and helping like they were your Own.
So cool to witness, how Black love is supposed to Be.
Brotha loves their Queen, Sista loves their King.
This is a shout out, a thank you for all the things we've been Through.
I wouldn't be who I am, where I am, if not for you Two
All I had were sisters but needed a couple Brothers.
This piece is for you LaMar & James; it's strictly for my Ni**a's.

Thanks for Listening

Everyone has something to discuss, something
to
get off their Chest.
Sometimes it's an everyday complaint; damn
just give it a Rest.
Sometimes you want to be heard, even if
there's no Solution.
You want someone to hear you out, even if half
paying Attention.
Not much effort is needed, to listen to a short
Story.
It's important to them, but to you it's probably
Boring.
Not everyone is built, to hear another person's
Concerns.
Listen up pay attention cause one day it'll be
your Turn.

The Black Mother

Sista all by herself no help raising her Kids.
Barely have the strength to cook dinner, working two Gigs.
Deadbeat dad has another man raising his son, never claiming his seed.
Not until the kid grows up, does well, makes it to the league.
She tells the deadbeat, "We don't need you, don't even bother."
"His coach has been here from jump, he's more like his father."
Single Sista is the Mom but also playing the daddy Role
She never complains, holds it down, that's all she's ever Known.
Mom and kids doing well, always had one another.
There's no better gift to have, than a Black Mother

The Definition of My Sister

My sister is the one that cares more than any other.
My sister is the one who's the protector of her Bigger Brother
My sister is the one who has your back when the chips begin to fall
My sister is the one who knows what to say, because she's seen it all.
My sister was the little pest before she became much older.
My sister is all grown up, so her voice is now much bolder.
My sister always keeps it one hundred, and never ever pretends.
My sister is just not my sister, but she's also my Best Friend

The joy of being me

No one understands me like I do
No one can feel my pain like I do
No one can brighten a day like I do
No one can make me smile like I do
No one has the great friends like I do
No one has the strength to keep fighting like I
do
No one feels passion like I do
No one can love deeply like I do
No one feels the Joy each morning like I do
Learn to love yourself, as much as I do

The Joy of Fatherhood

Not really a teenager, but not really full Grown
When I became a young and proud father of my Own
My son, my little dude, my twin, my Rock
Memories of time in the shop, getting our crops Chopped.
A baby is new to the world, no sense of direction not even a Clue.
Choose the right path so it's your steps their proud to Peruse.
Own up to your child, it's yours make that Claim.
Don't have your baby growing up, with two last Names.

You have earned this piece of Joy

You have earned this sunshine in your life.
You have earned the great friends you have.
You have earned the right to laugh daily.
You have earned the right to be hugged.
You have earned the right to be cared for
You have earned the right to shed a tear.
You have earned the right to see a better day.
Embrace it all... you've earned it.

The Joy of Life

Our goal is to celebrate life and the Beauty of it.
Make love your joy, grab those days you'll never forget.

Our energy stays on ten... spirit high with a bright smile.
You can see us coming not from a few blocks.
but from several miles
A queen just told me recently Happiness is the best outfit.
Look at our smile, look at our glow, can't you tell we click.

The Numbers Game

You know the numbers I'm talking about, 7, 8, 9, 10... ok pay attention

We all know people who are 10's and we know some 7's. Which one are you truly, think about it.

Ok 7's & 8's are unique in their own way, I will explain throughout this. Many people consider themselves a 10, but in all honesty their closer to a 9 or 8, here's why. 10's have been spoiled most of their lives by what they see in the mirror along with the constant reminder from others. Most 10's are shallow, not much substance attached, well not until later on in life when their reduced to almost an 8 and figure things out. Hardly ever will you see two 10's together, sometimes a 10 and a 7 or a 9 and an 8. You see 10's don't want competition they enjoy the spotlight, a 10 can carry that 8 around just to let people know who's really turning heads. Now you take a 7 for instance, 7's are cool, humble cause they know their a 7, the mirror reminds them every day "Damn I'm just a 7"...

it's ok though cause 7's can rise up.

The 7's & 8's have reality face them all the time; it's not bad being a 7 so chill. The 7's will be the caring passionate ones; you see 7's don't have the wiggle room like 9 or 10's. The 10 can get away with a few things for a while, but 7's aren't so fortunate. You see the 7 are always the unselfish type, giving their all to feel just a little special.

Ok here we go, a 10 with a stank attitude is easily reduced to a 9, if that 10 never changes, then the 10 will stay a 8 forever. 10's however can recover from being reduced to a 8, after a few years of troubled times and broken hearts, a 10 can rise up, you see when that 10 played the wrong person and it backfired. A 10 will look for that 8 or 7 just to play it safe, its ok cause now that 10 got a crazy dose of reality. Some 10's can make it as a couple, when they either started out young together, or they both felt the hard times and recovered and bounced back to being great 10's.... hey some 10's will never change ..Now some 10's think they might even be an 11 or 12... ok whatever that's why their always searching....ok Back to the 7's & 8's, they are the ones who will put in the work, I'm talking emotionally and physically etc, they will hold it down when things get hard, you see a 7 can rise up just by personality alone. The 7 can rise up with just a little help with their presentation/appearance and become a 8 or 9. The 7's never stop working on things. But there's nothing worse than a 7 with a stank attitude or a 7 rolling around acting like a 10....please, that stank attitude 7 will drop to a 5, 4 so fast.

You ever see a 10 rolling with a 7 and looking so happy, and wonder how in the hell did that happen, well the 10 had been through some shit and the 7 was there to pick up the pieces and repair that 10's heart. Now the 10 has a smile that can never be erased.

Now what are you ? I'm a 7, working on becoming an 8 0r a 9

Very Humbled

I'm very humbled by the journeys I take.
What makes me who I am... be it Bad or Good
is experiences.
Through experience you learn
Life is a daily lesson.
I'm a student every day paying attention.

Desire to be Humble

Blessed with amazing looks, catching the eye of both men and women. How do you react when such attention is bestowed on you on a daily basis?

Do you smile and say, "thank you" when that compliment is given, or do you react in such a way to quietly put out the vibe "Yes I'm very Beautiful"? Does it really matter how you're perceived by others, and do you honestly care?

Give it some thought, would you receive more attention from a humbled response or by a look by saying "Yes I'm the shit"

Let's see here

Beauty, that's a true Blessing, not every couple can produce a beautiful child, sometimes that child is only beautiful to family members only, let's be real about that. So, any person with amazing beauty was just plain lucky.

Wealth ... hard work, determination and drive can make your life and others in your family financially secure for a lifetime.

Wealth can also be handed down from previous generations and with wealth you can select the neighborhood to live in which will also have a better education system. Do people honestly think poor people enjoy being poor/hungry and even less educated. With some education comes better opportunities to succeed in life and there goes the upper class of living for constant generations on

Intelligence.... Comes from applying yourself to better yourself, also greater educational circumstance, also being Blessed with a brilliant brain.

Egos can be depleted in the drop of a hat, the loss of beauty, wealth, even intelligence can be taken away, then what are you left with.

Maybe a true friend if your Blessed to even have one, or did you push them all away with you craving for attention.

We are very fortunate to become a part of any goodwill, Beauty, Wealth or Intelligence.
Therein lies the Desire to be Humble.

Walking with a smile

I try not to be bitter but learn instead.
48

I want people to see my smile and not the disappointment
in my face.

I choose to walk my walk the way I know how.

Whoever wants to walk beside me.
They must do it with a smile....
Holla

The reason for writing

I write because I love to reflect on the times of life.
Times of so many good days and days of so much strife
Days when my heart is filled with hurt and sorrow.
Days when I just can't wait until tomorrow.
Days when I'm filled with so much Joy
Days reflecting back to when I was just a little boy
Days when I felt things couldn't get any better
Days when I was writing my first love letters
I write because I'm where I'm supposed to be
Loving myself and those who allow me to be Me

Dry Tears on a Pillow

Lying in bed, with heavy thoughts on the
Brain
Wondering somehow, to find the strength to
Maintain.
Up in the early morning, right before the sun
comes.
Thinking about lost best friends and missed
loved ones.
Tears refuse to fall, no need to wipe your Tears
No one can see you, so why you lying in Fear
It's not a person, who just refuses Cry.
It's just a Black man protecting his Pride.

Chapter 2
Love
"Doesn't take much to make me happy"
(Emotions)

Painted Picture

You painted this picture I never thought would become a part of my life ...never
believed it could happen to me
You painted a picture of Love, Compassion, Spirituality Warmth Care & Concern.
You became that ear that listens closely when I needed someone to hear what was
concerning me.
You became that Spiritual connection that reminds me daily everything is going to
be just fine when you trust in the Word and in God
You became a warm place to relax my mind and body after a long day
You painted a person of concern to show compassion to whatever I had gone
through in the past, that with you there would never be a need to doubt.
Then you painted a picture of what a real and true friend is all about
You painted a picture of falling in love isn't as scary as some might believe.
What a beautiful picture you've painted
It's our time Babe so let's frame it

A Jack & a Jill

She travels the country, He travels the Hood
She travels to places where he wish he Could

Her family consists of many, like in the Hundreds
His family is about fifty, mainly his boys and play Cousins

He thinks to himself, is it jealousy or just Envy
Is she cool where she's at, or could she trade places with Me
A tale of two people from different Backgrounds
Wondering if opposites can attract, dancing together with a different
Sound

A Love never Lost

What we had many years ago was a Joy we could never Forget.
We laughed hard and loved hard but argued quite a Bit.
Too young to understand, filled with bitterness and Jealousy.
When you placed my issues in front of me, I still refused to See.
Loving you for twenty plus, never lost that feeling, never got Tired.
Loving you for that many years, it seems our love can never Expire.
Through the years we lost contact and didn't talk as Much
Your kids were like my kids, and they continued to keep in Touch
Thank you for helping me grow and setting the bar so High.
Even through all the craziness, you were there by my Side.

A part of you

I listen to your Smile
I see your Soul
I see your Spirit
I hear your Walk
I see your Heart
I feel your Grin
I feel your Laughter
I see your Touch
I feel your Scent
If none of this makes sense, think about it.
There's no other way to explain other than
Every breath you take in, I'm right there trying to get a piece of that
fresh air.
Every time you begin to grin, I try to complete the laugh before you
can show off your
beautiful smile
Every time your emotions get the best of you, I'm wiping my eyes
before your tears begin to fall.
I want to be the Beginning, Middle and the End; I want no space
between us. I want to soak up every piece of Sadness, Joy and Laughter
that comes your way.

A Peaceful Evening

A peaceful evening a relaxing conversation
No drama talk.... easy to keep my attention.
Your soft voice.... your almost quiet giggle
Your smile was consistent as if you were being tickled.
Your smooth personality you always seem to possess.
Helps me unwind to relieve a day of any stress.
On the couch side by side as we watch TV
Thinking to myself, next to her is where I'm meant to be.

A Reason to smile

Trying to find the words to express the happiness you sent my Way.
My smile has a winning streak that continues Every day.
Trying to figure out what you see in me that has you being so Polite.
I'm so grateful that you looked my way, not once but even Twice.
Maybe it's God's Blessing that had you cross my Path.
Cause every time we see one another all we do is smile then Laugh.
I don't know what the future holds, but I'm wishing it's with You.
Your more than a fairytale, you're like my dream come True.

A Vacancy

There's room in my heart... there's a Vacancy.
If you listen closely, you'll understand, you'll See.
A heart beating with much passion, come closer so you can Hear.
A heart that will pull you in, to help escape all your Fears.
Only space for a special someone, not everyone is presented a Key.
Maybe a person with a warm Soul, that needs to feel at Ease.
Come inside get a good feel, is this what you always dreamed Of
A heart with concern, warmth, protection and so much Love
Open up your Soul, don't worry about any Pride.
If your eyes water up, then both our hearts begin to Cry.
There's a vacancy in my heart, for someone who's reaching Out.
Come inside my heart, cause there's so much to talk About

Be who you are

Sometimes people are who their
supposed to be

So someone else can walk up to them and
say

"Your exactly

what I was looking for"

Because of Him

You came along at such a perfect time.
It was a time when I needed something
wonderful...
There you appeared.
Somethings can't be explained...
That's why I'm such a believer in Fate & Faith.
I'll just give him credit and say God is good.
Cause he Blessed me with you.

Black Love Scene

Today was our day..... all alone just us two
We played it by ear....not sure on what we would do
Nothing came to mind no specific plans.
We just laughed ... giggled as we held hands.
Other couples walking around .... I know we were the cutest.
The way people glanced...obvious we were the smoothest.
We walked around like royalty Beautiful Queen , Protective
King
Black love was on display.... such a beautiful Scene

Day Dreaming

Quiet times just us two, all alone doing what we do.
Sunrise mornings on the beach... taking in God's Beauty
Strolling hand in hand, no one in front of us.... no one in
our way
Listening to classic jams.... Luther and Marvin Gaye
It's just us, so the ocean's a big ass puddle.
Let's grab a blanket.... squeeze closer.... let's cuddle.
Our eyes are closed so we can paint the perfect scene.
We're taking a noon nap, trying to finish this peaceful
dream.

Days without you

Days without you I miss your pretty brown Eyes.
Days without you I miss your soft brown Thighs.
Days without you I miss your gentle Touch
Days without you I miss your smell, that means so Much.
Days without you I miss your smile that brightens my Day.
Days without you I miss you saying, "Let's go to my place and Play."
Days without you I miss your soft juicy Lips.
Days without you I miss being in the shower, grabbing those Hips.
Days without you..... I miss

Diggin On You

The first time I saw you, I can't put my hands on the exact Date.
It was just many years ago... somewhere around Oh Eight
I'm digging on everything you say.... it's just your smooth Mental.
So every time I'm touching you... I'm a little nasty but super Gentle.
Trying every day to keep you happy.... keep your smile Going.
You got me girl... cause everyday my smile is always Showing.
I'm telling the truth about you and my constant Smiling.
You're the shit because I can't stop fucking Writing.
Diggin on You

Dime Piece

Just happen to be walking looking straight
ahead when I noticed a Dime.
Her Beauty was on point even though I seen
her up close just one time.
This Beautiful woman I only seen once has
turned into such a Mystery.
I still feel her warm presence from the first
time she stood next to me.
I'm moving towards her kinda slow... but with
good intentions.
Just to let her know I won't stop until I get her
undivided attention.

Emotional Flow

Met this beautiful Sista dealing with a heavy Heart.
She had something on her mind, but didn't know where to Start.
I could tell she needed a hug, just a soft Embrace.
Nothing to scare her off, just wanted her to feel Safe.
I felt her body tremble and noticed a few Tears.
Her body language showed no resistance not an ounce of Fear.
Holding her hand as she discussed the Situation.
She began to open up without any Hesitation.
Giving her a kiss on the neck as we parted Ways.
Telling her, "Maybe we'll cross paths..... again someday"
"Thank you" she replied," In helping me in ways you don't even know."
"I'm feeling better" she said "with my Emotional Flow."

Everyone Deserves

Everyone deserves something nice in life.
Everyone deserves something beautiful.
Everyone deserves a piece of Joy to come their way.
Everyone deserves a mentor or a life coach.
Everyone deserves that God sent Soul of a person to love
them.
I can't speak for everyone.
I just consider myself the Blessed one
Because I have you

Eyes on you

Had my eyes on this girl, she never had a clue.
Been looking her way for years, way more than two.
So humble she is ...always smiling, not knowing her beauty
So pleasant with a cool demeanor, never seen herself as a cutie.
I told myself I'm stepping next time I'm in her presence.
I been scoping her for years, had her under surveillance.
Always felt the vibes that she wasn't out of reach... not too far.
Even if she wasn't in my sight, I had her on my radar.
Finally, I saw her out one night.... kickin it with friends
I'm about to step to her now, let the dialog begin.

Falling in Love

Falling in love isn't something you always see on the big screen.
It's a feeling that makes your Soul, just want to break out and sing.
Love is an Action word and not just a figure of speech.
It's a feeling that you can't buy or not even teach.
Love can be viewed by others as you walk hand & hand.
Love gives another person's heart, such a soft place to land.
Love can come along when you never have a clue.
But loving the right person is something I always wanted to do.

Finally

Finally, I found someone who hears my heart.
Finally, I found someone who sees my Spirit.
Finally, I found someone who visions my warmth.
Finally, I found someone who feels my Passion.
Finally, I found someone who listened to my Cry.
Finally, I found someone who took a chance on Me.
It's about damn time, but finally.

Free to Fly

You knew I had a path to a certain place.
You knew when and how I wanted to achieve it.
I never wanted to be held down or led off course.
I never asked for a ride along
You just happen to hop on board.
Don't clip my wings to keep me from flying.
I just want to be free to soar at my own pace.
If this is not for you, I'm cool with that.
Just move aside so someone else can provide a softer landing.
My journey is toward Happiness.
Just let me be free to fly.

Humble Couple

We go through life hoping to find that perfect Match.
Some would call it, our idea Catch.
People sing that lonely sad song Why Me
Problem might be that person in the mirror that they See.
Sometimes we see the great things in people that others fail to see.
Through the years I just chose the person I felt that was right for me
I see so many couples Blinged out Flossed out trying to Impress.
I try to stay in my lane to skip & avoid all that financial stress.
At times my girl and I can barely rub two quarters together
We don't have much to spend, but we've always had our togetherness.

I got you

You're a bad ass beautiful queen who deserves so Much
Let me start off with a "Good morning Beautiful" a soft kiss
a gentle Touch
Next to you this morning is where I'd like to Be.
Spoiling you the minute you wake up, cause it's you I choose
Please.
Don't say a word, relax... lay there ...continue your Rest.
If I know you like I do, I shouldn't have to ask, no need to
Guess.
Before you get up... let's play, remove those covers.
Like I said earlier, relax... lay there, I got this... I'm taking
over.

I know I'm not perfect you say

Your beautiful caring and compassionate
Your Spirit is warm, touches so delicate.
Your always leaned up on me, very affectionate.
I'm not perfect you say.
Getting to know someone has its stages.
Moments with you just adds a couple more pages.
I'm not perfect you say.
I'm not complaining, I dig your curves.
Never boring so I enjoy your swerve.
I'm not perfect you say.
If you were ...then where would we be
You took a chance on me.
So I was granted this opportunity
Mmmmm so you say your not perfect.

I Love you

Thank you for being there.., always by my Side
I'm not perfect... I learned to swallow my Pride
Having you one day say yes and accept my
Hand
Has always been my goal... my Dream.... My
Plan
My heart says go for it, it knows what to Do
I hope I'm in your future; I'll leave that up to
You

I love you Girl

I need a Fix

Trying to start off my day, but it's moving at a slow Rate.
I need a boost of energy now; I don't have time to Wait.
Something to wake me up or perk me up, a kick or a Boost.
Something to get me going, I've got so much shit to Do.
I remind my girl to hook me up, she's also my Supplier.
I need it right now baby, before I get Tired.
It's on its way she says, I found your Fix.
She was right on time, with her beautiful morning Pics.

I Remember When

I remember when my friend and I talked about broken relationships and unfulfilled loves.
I remember when we would hang out for no other reason...... than just because.

I remember when the conversations were different, and not about being chased.
I remember every piece I put out... seemed to have its place.
I remember when my friend, became a close friend, like it was something meant to be.
Like you were who you were back then, and I was just me trying to be me.

I want to love Deep

I would like to someday meet someone I can spoil with my words of comfort, touch of pleasure, be able to know when something is wrong and already have the solution before she can even begin to tell me what she's going through. I want to give her a safe place to believe in. I want to be able to give her the Joy that she thought she could never receive.

I want to do it all not because she's my girl or she's so fine, but because she's so deserving of happiness being fulfilled.

I want her to know I believe in her more than she believes in herself. I want to love her with so much emotion to the point I tear up just as a way of saying thanks for coming into my life.

I want us both to have that deep emotional connection as to always feel, God is good cause he Blessed me with you. I want a girl that her demeanor says she's very happy with her Soul Mate ... when other women can whisper "Really"? and she can whisper back "Yes Really"

That's the girl I want to Love

If you're free Tonight

If you're free tonight come on Through
Let me show you my time is all about You
If you're free come on through Tonight
Let me feel you, taste you and hold you Tight
If you're free tonight come on Through
Let's lie in the bed, & play with each other till Two
If you're free tonight come on Through
Let me undress you slowly till I see your Birthday Suit
If you're free tonight come on Through
Let me please you so I can ask, "Baby is that Yo Juice"

Just because you said Hello

You got my immediate Attention.
I didn't wander off, I didn't talk, just Listened.
Just because you said Hello
I could tell there was something you wanted to Share.
You didn't know me, but my vibe showed I Cared.
Just because you said Hello
I listened about your ups & downs twist & Turns.
About not trusting others was the biggest Concern.
Just because you said Hello
Your mind seems in a much better Place.
You said Hello without invading my Space.
Just because you said Hello

Just for Me

My Lady knows how to comfort me & Complete Me
My Lady knows how to Touch me just to Tease Me.
My Lady knows how to Share with me and also Care for me
My Lady knows how to Listen just to confirm she's there for
me.
What a Special Lady I have
She Never leaves my side
Always next to me.
What a wonderful gift I have
She's everything
She's just for me

Looking Forward

I'm looking forward to just holding your hand as we watch
television or walking in the mall.
I'm looking forward to holding you in my arms as we stretch
out on the couch.
I'm looking forward to giving you a well-deserved full body
massage from head to toe,
I'm talking scalp to pinky toe.
I'm looking forward to the scent of your beautiful body....
I'm just looking forward.

Lonely Girl

Sitting at the table with her girlfriends on a night out
Trying to get a feel what the nightlife is all about
Never really had the chance to meet any fun guys
Been a homebody her whole life, in the house being shy
Brother approaches her table and ask may "I have this dance"
A little nervous but thinking, this might be her only chance
The night is just about done, when he ask "can I get your number"
Thinking to herself, he's fine I just might invite him over
Waking up the next morning with company she's never had before
Thinking to herself, I wasted years and money on these Motherfucking
Toys

Lose Focus

The beautiful work God has done by creating the Black woman
Has caused many of men to stop stare and pay Attention

Not much is needed to turn heads and gather a man's Stare
But it takes some preparation, determination and a little Care

No matter how much effort you place and how hard you Try
There's always another woman looking to catch your man's Eye

Going shopping with pajama pants and a doo rag at the Store
Oooops but who do you see, the nigga you danced with the night
Before
Telling your girl "I didn't see it coming what happened to Us"
Your man seen it coming, he just lost Focus

Lost Beauty

Beauty can be created, but we all know it's being Blessed
Only the believers who understand that, will always easily Confess

A beautiful smile with no emotion, is a deflector of some hidden Pain
Trying hard to keep the beauty up, hoping to erase the Shame

Be thankful you were selected and humbled you were Chosen
Not everyone can be beautiful when your spirit is always Broken
Telling everyone your beautiful saying it often and Loud
Is just a woman with no substance and a pretty face lost in the Crowd

Love reconnected

The beginning was nice and fun we were always on the go
Being around one another was nonstop... so we refused to take it slow
Your place my place we just made it work ...no matter the place
Some said it was too fast, but we enjoyed our love... our pace
Somewhere along the way we stumbled off course and lost our love
Wishing we could go back to the way things were... and once was
Missing you daily nightly and weekly ...trying to recapture our early
steps
Thinking if given another chance, we could make it right ...with no
regrets
Let's give it a try... a chance ...one last opportunity
Let's see if your heart pounds fast... like when you first saw me
Let's reconnect, be better friends ...a more loving couple.
Let's reconnect the way we know how.. this time we won't stumble.

Love

Love is a feeling that always says yes.
Love is the Joy that rises when things had become so Low.
Love is something that you should look forward to
Love is something you can't be scared to take a chance on
Love is something you shouldn't mind sharing.
Love is something you can't be mad at when you feel it let you down.
Love is the word that's your best friend when you can't find any other comfort.
Love is that soft word heard from someone when you know "they" meant that shit.
Love is the caring word spoken to someone when you know "you" meant that shit.
Love is the hug that came at the right time.
What is love to you
Figure it out, Embrace it.
I do it on a daily
Cause I love it

My Addiction

Never once did I think I would become an Addict.
That everyday fix that says you must have It.
It's that smile.. it's that Giggle.
It's that uncontrollable laugh without being Tickled.
It's that silliness we always seem to Share.
It's that loud restaurant laughter that sometimes brings a
Stare.
It's you becoming my best friend my Sidekick
It's me knowing what makes you laugh, what makes you
Tick.
It's you Babe I'm crazy about, pay Attention.
You're the reason I smile, you're my silent Addiction.

My Angel

Morning kisses I wish I was there to give you

89

Late night love making just so I could feel you

Lunch time phone calls to let you know I'm thinking of you

Weekend plans so I'm always next to you.
My Angel

My Favorites

You're my favorite fruit that leaves the taste of something so
sweet
You're my favorite color that blends so well against my
proud skin tone
You're my favorite shape to hold and cuddle next to
You're my favorite voice to hear when I need someone to
hear my pain
You're my favorite strength to hold onto when I begin to fall
or lose my balance
You're my favorite friend which is my best friend
You're my favorite love story to start this journey with
Your just my favorite

My Heart

My heart is always filled with thoughts,
not my brain but my heart.

I want my heart to smile every day and it's
always up to me.

I always want a reason to write.

Thanks for giving me a Reason

My Queen

This morning I woke up caught a vibe and had to see what I could do
Every morning I wake up the first thing I do is think of you
About hanging out doing fun shit that couples do
It might sound corny but an hour after your gone I'm already missing
You
The way we vibe there's no pretending our shit feels legit... feels true
Every time you sit next to me, I'm stuck on you like crazy Elmer's Glue
Well sexy I got to get back to work;
I hope you think of me the way I
think of you

Never Nervous

Being your man has been a Joy
And not once was I ever Nervous
Because you are such a Humble Lady
Being around you I was never Nervous
Because all you ever wanted was to be loved
Because showing Love was the only thing I could afford
I was never Nervous
Never once did you say buy me this or take me there
It just made me want to give you the world
Just because of that I was never Nervous
Falling in Love, sharing my Soul and calling you My Everything
Makes it easy to say these special words always
And never be Nervous

Our Journey

Two little kids just not happy with what the mirror Shows
Other kids being cruel .....always throwing low Blows
Self-esteem not high, trying to find someplace to Hide
We took so much abuse,,,,,cause we couldn't find any Pride
As we got older,,,, our looks began to Change
We look different now, but our hearts remained the Same
Thank God those days are over, glad they didn't Last
We are forced to stay humble cause you never forget the Past
Our Journey

Path of Love

I sleep with a smile when the last voice I hear is yours
Its confirmation that the choice I made, isn't just mines.....
but ours
A beautiful sista you are, let's make no doubt about it
The love we have is ours, so let's secure it
My evening aren't complete.... until you safely walk into my
arms
I need to feel it in your soul, that this world has given you
no harm
I need to see it in your smile that you know I love your every
step
With every professional or sexy stride, it's your path that I
protect
A Queen... My Queen you are each and everyday
You coming into my life is what I prayed

Perfect timing

You came along when I needed a special friend to lean on
You didn't know it then, but my feelings for you had been for so long
It's your beauty ..your smile ..your scent.. your touch
It was long over do, it's what I needed so much
Dim the lights you suggested, it's cool I don't care
No Babe ...I need them on a little longer, more time to stare
Thanks for coming through, when so much was on my mind
When you said "Baby I'll see you later" was perfect Timing.

Prayers Answered

You came along when I didn't expect to see you
You grabbed my hand said follow me... sort of like a rescue.
So many days I was hoping to find peace and happiness.
Life had been hell, countless hours of endless stress.
You came into my world and took on my problems.
Told me Babe we got this ...with God's help we'll solve them.
I'm much calmer now, I feel I can finally breathe.
Holding you in my arms, praying you'll never leave.

Queen

What a pleasure it's been to have you as my Queen
We're never at odds, God placed us on the same team.
You look your taste your smell your touch.
It's that evening appetite I've been craving since lunch.
My excitement started to grow inch by inch.
Having you walk in with basically nothing under that London Fog
trench.

Seeing You Again

Good morning pretty lady hope your day is going well.
I'm digging you somewhat.... I'm sure you can tell.
When I first saw you.... I couldn't believe my eyes.
I was peeping your smile ...your grace... even your body size.
Seeing you the second time.... asking your name was a must
before I let you go.
I had been practicing for months.... to surprise you with my
next hello
I was hoping to run into you...please just once more.
There you were before my eye.....leaving the grocery store

Seeing you for the first time

I had a feeling, a vibe from the first time I seen her Smile.
I wanted to see her again, but it would be a While.
Just by chance we happen to cross paths once More.
I knew it was her, I recognized that smile as I walked through the
Door.
Conversation was cool, kept it simple, pretty Casual.
Every subject we discussed, wasn't odd, seemed Natural.
Through time she opened up and told me about her Journey
This woman is something special, spilling her life's story to Me.
Since that reconnection of smiles, feels so good to be near Her.
Something in my heart won't let go, of what I feel for Her.
With every pic she sends, she's happy always Smiling.
That becomes my added motivation, to keep on Writing.

Sexy Lady

Every time you begin to speak, I'm all focused ready to listen.
Your words sound like my words, so I'm paying close attention.
Watching you walking around so beautiful I can't keep my hands to myself.
Your cool with my touching & tasting, your always "Hey just be yourself."
Our dinners are so pleasant, so peaceful, quiet times just us two.
Never quite satisfied with my meal, because my appetite is all about you.
Sexy Lady...thank you for your time taste and your feel.
I'm not trying to scare you off, but I think our shit is for real.

She Doesn't

She doesn't have to have it all, to be just Right.
Just be in my corner when things get Tight.
She doesn't need that knockout body to keep me Satisfied
Just be able to wiggle that apple, from side to Side.
She doesn't need to be the best ever, at showing her Talents.
Just when our time comes, show me there's no Limits.
She doesn't need to give in to my every Wish.
Just place me on your nightly dream List
She doesn't need to give me much More.
Just be the one, I've forever waited For

Smiling Again

Smile so beautiful and once again shining Bright.
Confirmation that her life is in order, and things are now Alright.
Crazy days are now in her past, as she looks towards the next Day.
No more sad times, when all she could do was Pray.
It took a while to get there, but she finally built up the Courage.
Friends see the new her, as she's free from mental Bondage.
Now a free woman, you can sense it in her Spirit.
No more bullshit will be taken, that you can best believe it.

Smiling while sleeping

I slept with a smile... cause all I thought about was you.
There was no disturbance... HELL, I slept right through.
When I close my eyes, you're on my mind.... and it takes me to a happy place.
My heart can rest, it feels at ease, it's now rescued... it feels so safe.
It's like the perfect dream you never want to end ..it just has to keep going
If you were to catch me sleeping... eyes closed my smile is still showing
When the morning arrives, I'm kinda sad, somewhat disappointed.
Even though I still think of you, my thoughts are sometimes interrupted.
The best part of my day is the evenings... when I'm finally next to you.
Hours later the next chapter of sleep begins, so my heart will be consumed.

So Complete

Such a Beautiful piece of work you are to Me.
So natural so complete, other women can't even Compete.
Smile is so radiant, like a child opening up his favorite Gift.
My focus stays on you, never ever wanting to Shift.
Body placed together very soft but also very Tight.
Gives me plenty motivation, to try and please you throughout the
Night.
Digging you it's about the physical but also about the Mental
Added motivation is, your walk, your wiggle, & your Jiggle

The view of you

It's the view of you that gets me through
To look at you is more than a glimpse .... It's a direct stare.
Others walk past me , they're not you..... they don't compare.
Trying to focus in ...never losing sight ..trying not to blink
Concentrating on you, never drifting off,,,, I'm always in sync
It's the view of you that gets me through
Close up or far away, it's your beauty that's always crystal clear.
Just like high school ,middle school, butterflies when your near
To be honest.. ..it doesn't matter if we never speak
I'm looking one last time, to get a final peak.

The Way I Love You

My purpose is to love you more intensely.
I want our love to grow as if there's no end to see.
I would like to hope the reason you smile is because of me.
I love you more than you know, that proves it's unconditionally.
I want to love you hard, but also very gently.
I want to love you each day so it's a love of consistently.
Loving you is so fun it's become like a hobby to me.
I want to love you just because... Maybe it's meant to Be.

There for You

We all have days we wish would just come and go Away.
Hard days when the best thing we could do ...was Pray.
Your not alone in this process, even though it might Seem
Remember the words once spoken ....."that we're a Team"
Because you opened up shared your life and stayed Humble
There's no way in hell, I would let you slip, fall or even Stumble.
Every day I wonder how your days is, sort of revolving around You.
Wiping your eyes of tears is something that I'm supposed to Do.

What If

What if I hadn't met you the sweet jewel of a woman 25 years ago
What if I hadn't known the travels and journey of this wonderful Queen
What if I hadn't heard her struggles her silent scream
What if I hadn't took the time to understand what she's truly about
What if all her words made me care for her without any doubt
What if I hadn't crossed paths with her to witness her new smile
What if I hadn't known she was this fitness guru that could run for miles
What if all the miles she was running was for a new beginning
What if all the people from her past failed to listen
What if she hadn't opened up about all her pain and sorrow
What if I had ran into her to let her know there's a brighter tomorrow
What if I had held on to you 25 years ago
What If

What we share

You came into my life, when I didn't even expect It.
You began to cross my mind, when I tried to not even let It.
You opened up your heart and exposed a personal part your Life.
Not all was sad, some was joyful, through that tunnel you seen the
Light.
What we have and what we've become only God knows where this is
Headed
The bond we have the times we shared has not once been Regretted.
I write about my smile and the smile I might be able to give You.
I write because having an Angel in my life, makes everything run
Smooth.

Something in common

Queen you are the jewel, that keeps me Smiling
Our energy is nonstop, so we keep on Striving.
Your Soul your Spirit is something beautiful I cling to
No one has the gift to keep me smiling the way that you do
It's your charm your grace your picture-perfect Face.
Only thing that keeps me from you is a few miles... all that Space
We have seemed to connect as if we went to grade school Together.
Our daily conversations always seem to make my days even Better.
Thank you Queen, for being who you truly Are
Your just a few minutes away, which really isn't that Far.

Something to Prove

Whenever I spend time with you... I'm happy never wanting to leave you
I just want to Cozy up...Cuddle ....anything to please you
Somedays I just want to pick you up... to show you I'm strong for you.
Stand in front of a raging bull or a crazy fool, just to protect you.
I just want to lay next to you all day, cause there's nothing better to do.
I want a shirt that says your name, so others will know I belong to you.
I been in search for love a long time, it's way overdue.
I can be a good man, I know this..... I have something to prove.
You came into my life at the perfect time ....cause God knew I needed you
You been in my life a short time, but there's no smile for me without you.

Should've Been You

I let the years go by never speaking up when you were always on my mind.
Never quite knowing what to say, never felt it was the right time.
Should've have been you a long time ago, I felt the connection.
You always gave me that smile, I punked out, being scared of rejection.
I let so many others distract me and come between my true feelings.
Should've been you cause everyday it's you ...that helps me erase my demons.
I'm trying to always place a bug in your ear.. give a little hint, trying to get a feel.
Trying to figure out at any moment, have you ever wondered about us, I'm just being real.
I just had to place it out there, cause it's never too late I guess never too soon.
Just wanted to let you know for a long time it should've been you.
Damn girl it should've been you

Special Someone

What a lovely sight of perfection I witness when I look at You
My Soul can stop searching; God knows I paid my Dues.
What a special woman she is, with a warm caring Spirit
My heart seems to connect with hers, every time I'm near It.
She's always smiling as if she invented Sunshine.
It's her way of saying, enjoy life cause time really Flies.
My dreams are no longer a dream, there coming close to being Reality.
Look at my Soul feeling special, as she's up on me.

"Swept Away"

Could it be true that she's as cool as she appears to Be?
Could it be true that she has her eyes focused on just Me?
Is it reality that this woman is as gorgeous, like the type you see across
the Screen?
Is it reality that this woman reminds me every day, that I'm her King?
Is this the woman that has taken away all the pain that I've Endured?
Is this the woman that reminds me daily that our bond is strong and
insured?
Yes, she made it plain, but sprinkled it with love for my eyes to See.
Yes, it's true, that this Queen, this spice of Beauty, swept me off my
feet.

Thinking of Him

The smile he presents me with everyday lets me Know
The previous day was a Blessed day... cause my smile still Glows.
Thinking of him because
He allowed my Soul to once again open Up.
He did it with the kindest words the softest Touch
Thinking of him because
He cherishes the Joy I bring him Daily
Looks at me constantly refuses to turn Away.
Thinking of him because
There's a place in my heart just for Him.
Our love is always on display, not for us but for Them.

Because I'm thinking of Him

The price of love

Love ... what is it...what does it mean what does it do.
It's that personal feeling you give someone or an emotion placed on you.
Love is the joy you can give out to others. Doesn't cost you anything. Loving
someone is free.
Love isn't judgmental, you accept that person for who they are and what they're
meant to be.
Love is beautiful when you can open your heart and bare your Soul
Just keep expressing your feelings and magical words will flow
Love is that warm heart, that soft embrace, the feel you get at the perfect time, that
gentle Touch
All Love cost you is the effort to smile and the passion to care, I told you, Love
doesn't cost you Much
The price of Love

You

You allowed me to be who I am, you allowed me to be free.
You showed me what love is about, you let me be me.
You hung in there when I was flat broke and didn't have a dime.
You hung in there when all I could ever afford to give you was my time.
So many others used me as something to sport or just as a Date.
My money was never long enough and they never found time to wait.
Every time you see me it appears to brighten your day.
You helped all those rotten memories fade and pass away.

Thanks

Thanks for giving me a chance when others wouldn't.
Thanks for loving me when others couldn't.
Thanks for holding my hand when others didn't care to
Thanks for being in my corner when others didn't dare to
Thanks for loving me Babe when others never thought
about it.
Thanks for thinking about love when others never talked
about it.

Thanks for Love

Tailor Made

So glad we became what we are. Only God knows what that is.
What we have is a unique bond, that decision was his
We never drifted too far to forget the times and smiles we use to share.
People will wonder what's up with us, let them talk ...let them stare.
I remember you saying my words to you were sweet and personalized.
Of course, they were my Queen, us never losing contact is no surprise.
Us just being who we are... has seemed to work... never seemed to fade.
Like I once told you, what we have special, it's tailor made.

Why Me Why You

Lately I been wondering Why Me Why You
Was it just love by chance or was it just a fluke?
You have continued to hold true to your every
word.
Demonstrating that love is something shown
and just not heard.
You saw something in me and I always
wondered what it could be
Maybe it was just something that many others
failed to see.
You listened to my Soul and heard it speak
loud.
Let's showcase our Love and show others how.

Chapter 3
Black Beauty
"Black Coffee no Sugar no Cream"
(Heavy D & The Boys)

A Visual

Do you ever have an image or a visual that
never seems to Fade?

It's that pretty face, her sexy voice, her smell,
you can never Evade.

Thinking about the first and the last time, you
witnessed her wonderful Smile.

Like a brand-new mother, holding her first
born Child.

A woman with Style, Grace, and with
complete Substance

Take a double look... try not to blink if you
ever get the Chance.

Light colored eyes that blends well with her
pretty brown Skin

Every time she's in my presence, I tend to stare,
again and once Again.

Beautiful Queen

A Beautiful Queen is not given that Title, she's
Selected.
She walks with Beauty and Grace, that's why
she's Protected.
It's just not her smile but also her demeanor.
She's the lady others look at, wishing they
could be her.
It's you, who carries that title.
The woman that makes the young ones say,
"see her, she's my idol"

Crazy Back

You know it when you see it.
It's not close to being fake .... Believe it.
It's that backside....that has a crazy curve
Yes, it is what you think, your visions not blurred.
It's that end table that nightstand ...a place to set your glass.
It's perfect from every angle, it's that beautiful black ass.
People searching and asking "where did she get it"
It's from the Motherland, Uganda, Zimbabwe... very authentic.
Guy's stare and girls notice when they see a crazy Back.
It's a perk... it's a plus... it's just a part of being Black.

Dope Wiggle

It's the shape it's that size.
It's the attention that captures your eyes.
It's the shift, it's the shake.
It's the constant double take.
It's the body part I call an Apple.
Take a bite just as a sample.
It's her strut, it's her walk.
Listen closely you can hear it talk.
It's the sundress silhouette.
Keep looking she's not done yet.
It's the high heels that make it rise.
It's the piece of fruit above her thighs.
You know what I mean, I'll keep it simple.
It's the way she walks, I call it a Dope Wiggle

Face of perfection

It's that face with a wonderful skin tone.
It's the face that the beauty starts from the bone.
It's the face that's blends well with her full lips.
It's a face that others ask for beauty tips.
It's that perfect nose that goes well with a diamond stud.
It's her smile when she wakes up and she's gorgeous just because.
It's her brown eyes that pull in so much attention.
No contacts were needed, they were beautiful from the beginning.
It's a billboard face, ideal selection.
It's a Black woman ...It's a Face of Perfection

She's So Gorgeous

Every time I'm next to her.... I'm trying my best not to stare.
It's an unmanageable task......... almost like a dare.
Thinking to myself, No way this woman is this damn pretty
Looking at her up close, she's a pretty picture .... like HD TV
I only know her just a little......trying to know her better.
I wonder if she even knows.... our names share the same letters.
Her skin is brown to perfection, Essence magazine glamor style.
We have a little in common ..... We share the same unique smile.
Her beauty never seems to leave... my daily thought process.
It's a craving to see her, it sounds crazy....maybe I'm obsessed
Gorgeous she is

Pretty Brown Eyes

To look into these eyes, you wonder about the past... the Journey.
Wondering what all has she been through... what all has she Seen.
Is there love in those eyes or much heartbreak and Disappointment?
Wondering has she found happiness and a desired Fulfillment.
I see beauty strength and a very compassionate Soul.
Knowing that things from the past had almost taken its Toll.
She's a new woman now, with a look you can't Deny.
She's a beautiful woman, with pretty brown Eyes.

Sista's with Freckles

Freckles on a Sista so different but also so Unique
If you've never seen it before, I request you sneak a Peek.
Rose colored stars with a pretty brown backdrop.
Matches well with a Halle Berry hair style, closely Cropped.
Sista's with freckles is like extra spice, to something that was already Delicious.
They know they stand alone, their beautiful, a rare breed, very Precious.
Sista's with freckles an added piece of her Beauty
She's a dime, a sexy Queen an all-world Cutie.

The making of something Beautiful

How gorgeous and sexy can a Sista really Be.
When she lets her imagination open up and run Free
The kinda girl that can gather looks from all across Town.
She's the type that can Smack it.. Flip it.. and also.. Rub it Down.
When describing her style and look, you can leave no Doubt.
She's the one brotha's at the club, stare and wonder About
Just a simple piece of elegance and fantastic Beauty
For you to open up your eyes and love what you See

Chapter 4
Pride

"You're a Slave to a page in my Rhyme book"
(Nas)

One hundred percent Soul

Taking the time to notice something so Beautiful so sultry
Has many people taking a glimpse....slight jealousy with strong envy
Soul Sista filled with strong confidence and PhD Intelligence
She's her own woman with her own rules
You could never figure her out... if you were given a hint... with several clues
She's about her people... her pride... her vision
Quiet please ... she's about to speak... pay attention
Start listening.
Don't be fooled by her Redbone skin tone.
Oh, She's black... and it's to the Bone.

100 % Soul

A Better Me

Who am I to point a finger or make judgment on anyone else?

I'm aware of my many flaws.

So each day is a journey towards a better me.

That daily journey begins when I walk away from the mirror.

Being Black & Proud

Walking down the street being Black & Proud
At times it feels like walking under a dark
Cloud
The hard looks from others is always easy to
See
Nothing but jealousy and pure Envy
They can buy our music and sample our Gear.
Walking in their direction brings out nothing
but Fear.
Trendsetters we are coming up with new
Inventions.
Being the first man on earth was God's
Intention
Never feel as if there's a dark Cloud.
Just keep walking, walking Black & Proud

Being Me

I don't want to be cloned, or be a copycat .. I enjoy me, different and all.
I might not fit the mold, but who said the "Idea mold" is shaped well.
Let me be different and loving and see where that takes me
Just let me be the "Remix "
I might be ok to some, but if you listen close, I bang louder .....holla

Let's be Black Again

Can you vision a duet with Marvin Gaye serenading to
Mary J
How about a smooth flow from Patti .. hooks by Biggie
Heart breaking song by Chaka, teamed up with Tupac
Cruising to the studio was Smokey, on his way to pick up
Aaliyah.
Was it a Dream that Left Eye had just finished a track with
Mike?
I believe it to be, like Whitney collaborating with Eazy E
Just like Natalie Cole, on tour opening for J Cole
Hey, let's get our people back.
To do a dope remix a crazy track.
Back from where it all began.
Let's be Black again.

Black Beauty

Black beauty walking down the street so Powerful.
Don't approach her crazy.... Be careful.
Figure always looking right, so close to being Perfect.
Body so amazing, as if it's written in Cursive.
Lips so full of beauty to add to a man's Temptation.
Just a natural gift, another one of God's Creations
Blonde coworkers looking as if it's not Legit.
Knowing their forced, to purchase this type of Shit.

Throwback Queen

Her look is beautiful... all natural skin ...so Clear
No makeup was needed ...no smudge... no Smear.
Her walk is with Substance, Elegance and Confidence
Her scent is like a magnet, closing the Distance with hard Resistance.
She keeps it real, always truthful never fake never Phony.
Calling out those who live through tv and never facing Reality.
A seventies throwback, carefree and free Spirit
Her unique style makes her adorable, also Different.
Loves her People her Pride her History.
Give her ten minutes time, pay attention, you'll See.
She's a throwback Queen, built from Within
She can recite our history from Beginning to End

Natural Queen

They say Beauty is in the eye of the Beholder.
But the touch of her beauty is better...If you can "Hold Her"
Some feel it takes some work to become a Queen.
Like add a little makeup... a little hair, know what I Mean
God taught us all to love ourselves for who we Are.
I've seen too many take hair... and makeup a bit too Far
I told my Girls, love yourself ...your made for a King.
You're Beautiful... your Black... you're a Natural Queen

Passion for my People

Passion for my color and my People
Will always be real, cause the treatment has never been Equal.
For eight years we had a brotha run this sick Nation
We claimed him as ours, even being half Caucasian.
Look in that mirror without any Shame.
Cause the color of your skin will never Change.
Equal rights and equal housing, that shit was just a Tease.
Should have known up front cause we built this bitch for Free.
Passion for my people I hold with so much Pride.
Cause it's that other man, who continues to tell us Lies.

Bronze Queen

Looking across the way I saw this Figure.
So gorgeous, looked as if it was a painted Picture.
Sculpted really nice, like a piece of fine Art.
In crowds of many people, she stands Apart.
Standing about six feet tall so hard to Miss
Looking like a real-life Hersey's Kiss
A real-life statue it turned out to be.
This Chocolate beauty reminds myself of me

Caramel So Sweet

So Beautiful she is, just like a Painted Picture
When describing her looks, kinda sounds like a Scripture.
So sweet So kind and also very Classy
So close to perfection, thinking to yourself This can't Be
Pretty caramel skin, something so hard to Miss
She taste so sweet, just like a after dinner Dish

Forgotten Fruit

Not too many Brotha's see beauty by having dark chocolate covered
Skin
They act as if it's something you can catch.. or maybe even a Sin
Back in the slavery days the Black man was considered the forbidden
Fruit.
Now it's the modern-day slave owner, who considers our Sisters
gorgeous and Cute
A person can choose happiness with whomever he sees Fit.
Just go back 200 years and it wasn't your dad or your brother cracking
that Whip.
Look in the mirror Brotha man and see if you can find some Pride.
All that shucking and jiving, just go someplace and Hide.
Black women come in different shades, don't forget about them my
Brotha.
If you want confirmation of their beauty, go hug your Mother.

Home Sweet Home

9 to 5 gets nothing but crazy looks stares and frowns.
Back home mad love... dap and continuous pounds
9 to 5 there's no one walking the halls... with my skin tone.
8 hours of fake smiles and hello's so I'm all alone
9 to 5 people in hallways whispering crazy statements.
Can't wait to get home where I feel much more safe.
Back home greetings are real eye to eye with a purpose.
Cause people look like him her and them just more diverse.

How many do you know

Let's see how many people of color you really know.
When you see them at work or the store, do you always say
hello.
Always saying "That's not me but my grandparents
Generation."
The only time a brotha has been in your home was on a
television.
Station
Never happy to mention a Black man's name I swear.
Unless you're in the closet looking for his jersey to wear.

<u>Seasonal Negro</u>

You ever walk past a certain individual, and they look at you as if you didn't exist You know what I mean, an individual that you can make eye contact with

You know the individual that you can speak to with a simple hello No matter if you say hello , hold open a door . You're still invisible.

There's something you need to consider. This mostly happens when "WE" people of a darker skin tone tend to waste our kindness and manners on the wrong person.

Most of the time the wrong person will have a much brighter skin tone than ours... see what I'm saying.... dig what I'm getting at....

Then all of a sudden, these lighter skin tone people begin to be extremely polite, tend to want to chatter a little more often. You ever wonder why these people become a chatterbox....

It's usually around the months of say August to February... or maybe every 4 years they become more in tune to your likes and dislikes. Those years can change from every 4 to every 2... depending on ..... well, you should have figured it out by now.

Let's go back to those months of August to February..... is this starting to ring a bell... Ding Ding.

We can most likely expect politeness, the care the concern during those periods of time, that time of the year.

One to never bite his tongue, so here you go if you have failed to see what's in front of you.

WE as in the darker shade of people are seasonal.... YES. Those are the months when there's no need to overdo it at work... give that extra smile. Betty , Heather and Chad will ask you "How's the family doing" "How was your drive in"

Plain and simple, we are what I call the Seasonal Negro. When there's a vote needed every (2) or (4) years, here comes Billy all of a sudden giving a damn..... Its election time and every vote counts, even yours Keisha & Jalen

Those months I spoke of earlier.... It's called the N.F.L. football season, you know, the sport that shuts a business down for every Sunday and is treated as if it's a holiday when the championship is being played. The N.F.L. just so happens to be roughly 80% made up of people of a darker shade than the general population....

It's amazing how Billy finds the need to ask about your fantasy football lineup EVERY WEEK, when back in April he wouldn't hold the elevator for you... it wasn't the season for you Bro.

Play close attention to when and how often that care and concern is distributed. Don't sleep on this, those refusals to speak back or walk past you without a simple head nod...

It's that silent "Not now N***@ not now.

Pay close attention as I always do.

I refuse to be a Seasonal Negro

Keeping it Real

Let's get to the point straight up... no more pretending.
You see what's going on, it's our physical hurt, you it's just your feelings.
Quick to make a statement about people when you never walked in their
Shoes
Get mad when we speak up, we get profiled, hell we've paid our dues.
Telling everyone that Donnell at work is your Black friend.
Get home telling your family "he's there because of affirmative action"
Don't give me that shit about everything being equal.
If you only have one black friend ...you don't care about my people

The Color of Us

The color of us can bring such a fuss.
Picking apart our own kind, losing our mind
The only race of people that judge one another
by skin tone.
Knowing deep inside.... when your Black it's to
the bone
Being so Black people say "he aint mixed with
shit"
Be it light skin... red bone. or blue black
When your black your still one hundred
percent legit
It's the color of us

Haters

Look at you always upset always Mad
Can't even fix your face …. everyday looking Sad
Looking at me every day wishing you had just a little of my
Swag
My mind works different than yours, so you'll never have my
Vocab
Don't like the way you look…. Get off your lazy Ass
You might have a couple things more than me but you're a
hater, so you'll never show Class

The Truth

Every month you gather up.... call a meeting all
happy,
Calling it a Pep, it's just the annual klan Rally
What's sad is a black man that's forgotten his
Roots.
Agreeing with Mr. Charlie, you Uncle Tom
...you Jigga Boo
First thing Monday morning can't wait to talk
the Score.
Acting like you know LeBron, he's my Nigga,
not Yours
Kap has half this country showing pride fist
highly raised.
While the other half is walking around pissed
off & red Faced

Chapter 5
Passion
"Still some quiver when I deliver"
(Chuck D.)

Time well spent

Haven't seen you in a while, it's been about a week, so it was long overdue
You're right, you said ...."so this weekend for sure .... I'll fall through."
After a couple of glasses of wine.. you felt relaxed body started to twitch.
Let's go upstairs so I can undress you... every few minutes whispering "switch."

Coming through on that evening play time started in the P.M.
After breakfast in bed... we're back at it, playing in the A.M.
Later in the day I was happy with three words you happen to choose.
You laid it on me heavy.... and said Babe....... "I miss you"

Twenty-Four Seven

Closing my eyes at night, just thinking of you
Never lost focus, because I woke up next to
you.
What a better way to start off my day
Than to have breakfast where we both just laid
Thoughts of you, and the day we first met.
All I envision is a continuous silhouette.
Can't wait for this long day to end.
Just to start off, with a brand-new beginning
My dream begins as you walk through the
door.
Let's make this a reality, just like the night
before.

Play Time

Beautiful Sista trying to find a way to relax and Unwind.
There's only one thing that crosses her erotic Mind.
Fun begins with teasing & many positions of fourplay.
She pulls me closer commands we do things her Way.
On my back being straddled by warm throbbing Thighs
Body being jerked & bounced like a rollercoaster Ride.
I ask my Babe to give me a count, she holds up three Fingers.
She replies, winded & out of breath, damn. . you're a
different type of Nigga.

Yummy

It's that desert I crave....something so beautiful that was
naturally made
Yummy
It's that pretty space below her waist that gives me a great
taste.
Yummy
It's that juicy candy.... a place to soak my face in.....feeling her
uncontrollable quivering
Yummy
It's her G spot for me to suck on.... for 45 minutes or until
I'm all done
Yummy
It's her trimmed nice treasure that gives us both much
Pleasure.
Yummy
There's no stopping me I do what I do, it's a hobby for me.
Yummy

Pleasure Provider

It's never a question of.... what I won't do
It's more of ....what you'll allow me to do
I'm your Dream Seeker
Your Flow Controller
Your Moist Maker
Your Splash Master
If you like what you hear
Shit even like what you see
Damn ....you know who I am
I'm that Pleasure Provider
Just Google Me

Our Time Spent

Straight from the heart to express the way I Feel
Always being honest.. so you can know what's the Deal
My eyes have been fixed on you... for close to a Decade.
Never wanting to scare you off.... So I kept quiet & down Played
You're so Beautiful so Sweet a complete spice of Joy.
Hoping I could satisfy you as a real-life Chocolate Toy
The passion was warm... erotic... gentle with much Spice.
I couldn't let you leave ...without making love at least Twice.
On your stomach you laid, it was reality no Dreaming.
It was your spot you said, it kept the moment Steaming.
It was a quiet peaceful night, no rain, no Storming.
You gave me five hours of pleasure... leaving at five in the Morning.

Drug of Choice

At times searching for that perfect High
She gives me a glimpse of that pretty brown
Thigh.
When I'm feeling down and kinda Low
She's right on time ,to give me that Blow
When I'm in need, of just a Taste
She tells me her candy, is below her Waist.
Mouth so full of pleasure, I lose my Voice
I just finished tasting, my Drug of Choice

Driving Force

Driving next to me I couldn't help but to notice a spectacular View.
Thinking to myself, damn if she pulls over my backseat has room for Two.
Thinking could it be you that has me headed in this Direction.
Seems like you're the one, who's going to be my evening Selection
Finally gathering her attention, I asked if she cared to take a Ride.
Her reply was "Yes nigga but only if you let me Drive."
By her style of driving, I could tell she was use to the Bounce
After thirty minutes with her behind the wheel, never once did she say Ouch.
After two hours of driving I asked for her name, I never had a Clue.
Her reply "don't look for me...Nigga I'll find You."

Greedy

Appetite never satisfied always wanting more
My hunger intensified as you walked through the door
I'm Greedy
Let me show you how hungry I am.. give me a few seconds
Hey there's a park over there
Go grab the blankets.
Just Greedy
My hunger is so about you, let's see if you can take it.
No pretend moaning.... shit there's no way you can fake it
So Greedy
My meal is you. I'm not going anywhere so slow down... stop running
My request is your kitty kat ..I'm not slowing down... so keep coming
So Greedy
Don't be all offended... stuck up ..like "damn oh wow".
If you understand my thought process, then you should know me by now.
Cause I'm just greedy.

Lady with a Crush

Lady telling her friend about a man she seen at the store.
Saying he's too fine to turn away from... too hard to ignore.
Friend suggest they go to the store, to see what he's all about
Looking at him she can tell he's a gym rat, can tell he works
out.
"That's him ...there he goes girl right over there."
"Damn Don't look too long try not to stare."
Telling her friend if she had one weekend just once chance.
She would call in sick maybe skip all her weekend plans.
She can't seem to forget this man ...refuses to let it go.
All she can think of
"GIRL THAT NIGGA JUST DON'T KNOW"

Lady looking for a night of pleasure

Bro I'm sick and tired of all these disappointments.
So I'm giving you a call…. trying to set up my next appointment.
Dude I know your booked out, months in advance.
I just need you to fix the desire in my pants.
Just trying to find a time to "come" and swing through.
I was telling my girlfriend about you… so now she wants to "come"
too.
I'm sure she'll enjoy coming, it's my time so she'll have to watch.
I know Your time is valuable…. cause I'm always on that clock.
I just pulled up, time to do what you do.
My girl is just here to watch, so don't charge me for two.
Damn bro you got my legs straddled around your waist.
I kept on bouncing, didn't slow my pace.
I'm holding on tight trying not to fall
Just keep doing what you do. Tapping every wall
Damn bro, you left me speechless, can't talk straight…. sounding
retarded.
I'm too exhausted now, told my girl…. "fuck that party"

Chapter 6

Thank You

"I wanna thank you for letting me be myself"

(Sly Stone)

My Aunties

God is so wonderful because he Blessed me with the 3 beautiful gifts.
I was born into the family of some very unique women, my Aunties.
My Aunt Lizzy, Clara & Verna Lee... God's finest. BEST EVER.
These remarkable women are my dad's sisters, sisters who love hard.
These are the women who carry the same skin tone as mine, these are the women who have the same blue ring in their eyes like my dad and myself, they are my strength.
They have been the best of friends since birth. They have prayed for me for almost 60 years.
They only allow me to walk up and give them a loving hug and kiss cause they're not about all that mushy stuff, I guess I get a pass. I can go talk ball games with one aunt.. she knows every sport, or I can walk and talk to my other Aunts cause they know the Bible from beginning to end and will toss out a scripture just to remind you how Blessed you truly are.
My cousins Evelyn and James also held it down for my Aunties and loving me as their little cousin. My San Antonio Cousins and family have been my strength from many miles away. Yes, I'm a Colorado resident but I'm actually a Texas kid born in a small town.
Thank you for being my strength, thanks for loving me, thanks for praying for me every day.

The Walkers

The Walker family, wow, I'm expressing my thanks throughout the years 40 plus and counting. From Britt, Ashton, Breezy & James II (Baby J) Paula and my Bro James, I'm not at this point in my life of happiness and humbleness if it hadn't been for all your support.

Thanks for loving me for the way I chose to be, thanks for allowing me the freedom to be loud and loving through the years.

James I already expressed my thanks in "Strictly for my Niggas" but you have been that brother at all the perfect times in this journey, from our football days, from my early days as a single parent to being asked and honored to be the Godfather to James II. Thanks for being that great part of the village that helped me raise my kids and thanks for letting me be a part of your kids lives

The list of thanks goes to Bro, with much thanks to your mom Ms. Cindy & Jerry. Ms. Cindy all we do is laugh and clown, thanks for calling me your son also. Cousins Mike & Spider and Hill... right on as well

The Hudson's

It all started 40 years ago when Lee (Leticia was just maybe 4 years old) when her and her sister Bobbi came into my life.

As the years went by and you became my little sister, you witnessed the growth of your brother Dex. Fast forward maybe to 1990 when I was introduced to Train (LaMar), since then you both have proven what the Christian walk looks like and displayed Black Love at its best. You both never judged, just always supported, never lectured me, just placed positive words in my ear.

Whenever I wanted to lose it and blast my verbal strong choice of four-letter words, Train just said

"Dex don't even trip with that"

Because you let me be me and continued to show me love as well as being a great support for my family throughout our times of sadness. I just have to say thank you both. Thanks for letting be the loud Uncle while watching Lenzi & Landri ball. You both just always laughed while I was the loudest at the games.

Train. Lee, Lenz & Landri thank you sooooo very much

Brother Manuel & Sis LaVon

Right on for so much. It's been 30 plus years that you've locked in and became a part of my family. From the time Mike wasn't even born the relationship was formed. Your folks treated me as a son as I feel my parents treated you and your family just as loving. When I lost both my parents my sisters and I knew who we wanted to play an important role in their Homegoing

You & Von stepped up and did so much and provided so much comfort.

From the times when our kids shared so many birthday parties to when I was on your security team walking you to the ring, to the times all we did is grub at your place.

Bro the love runs deep today just as it did 30 plus years ago.

I don't walk this path through life if it hadn't been for you and your family.

Valence, Manuel Jr, & Mike, Uncle Dex says thanks for making all the love our families.

shared happen. God is good Bro, every day we rejoice in his goodness.

Much Love

Paul

My brother

How else can I start a "Thank You" without saying your favorite phrase.

I'm just reaching out to say right on for 25 years and counting of a strong friendship.

Dude through God you became a permanent fixture in my life, many journeys in life we both have faced.

My brother, only if you knew how many times when you opened up your home to me to kick it watch games grub and just fellowship. Your hospitality was always right on time, little did you know many times years ago I was broke and starving but God made it that your calls came through to ease my Soul and fill my belly...lol

I remember back when Lebron was with the Heat and we were at your brothers, the game was over and you said "Dex grab a plate for you and your son" Bro my son and I tore up that chicken and my son's words were "Dad... Paul is a bomb ass cook" little did you know our fridge was empty that night.

With the love that you and your wonderful family has extended my way will always be a reminder on God's graces in life. Paul, you walk the walk, to witness the love of family, husband and wife and fatherhood always brings me Joy. To have the solid Queen by your side is a Blessing that I know you cherish.

Bro leaving the gym or leaving your crib from a ball game,
our words are always "Love you Bro"
Through God all things are possible, thanks for being there
at the right time, even when you didn't realize it.

The Browns

Brother Jarvis.... Hey Bro, from jump we made it happen as brothers. There was always something that held us tight like family.

Then to find out you and my Bro James were also like brothers, that's God working his magic to bring greatness together.

Thanks for all the hospitality you shown by letting me and my family feast at you and your wonderful wife's home.

When I was starving you told me with a stern voice, "Hey Nigga swing through so I can load you up" that moment... those times will forever stay strong to my Soul.

Good looking out, forever grateful.

My Best Friend Trina

T where do I begin to thank you for years of support
You stood by my side through the worst of times.
You not once tried to judge me, you just continued to love me.
We have a friendship, a special bond, a bond that can never be replaced. You're my sidekick, my breakfast buddy for close to 10 years. We have always kept it 100 even on times when I might not stay in contact as I should. You'll call me up, cuss me out... Telling me "D don't be disappearing on me nigga I need you" Only you have the green light to basically say "D what the fuck" That's what Best Friends do. Keep it real.
Not only have you been my Best Bud. Having you in my life you Blessed me with two wonderful niece's. your wonderful daughters. My Joys as well.
All we do is laugh and talk shit wherever we're at. Volume always at the highest level ...what we call "Nigga Shit"
People always stare but I think they're too afraid to tell us to shut up ... You're the shit girl. Always there for me I truly appreciate having you in my life.
Trina you are my BFF ... my T. My Running Red Feather
God is so good cause he Blessed me with you.
Love you girl.

Bee Harris

It was 1990 when I first submitted my first couple of writing pieces, this was something new to me and I wasn't sure how I did. Both pieces were on race slash sports related. It was back in the days of no cell phones, not even sure the internet was up then. I was a newly single dad living at my mom's when the landline phone rang, I answered and the lady on the other end said "hello this is Bee from the Urban Spectrum newspaper" to make a long story short she said 'I would like to submit both your articles in next month's issue".

I was overjoyed, never thought anything I would write would be published in a paper. Bee later asked who do I write for and what writing school had I attended. I told her this is the first time and I never went to school to write other than creative writing in High School. Bee said both articles were good, then offered me a job on the spot to be their sportswriter and told me how much they paid. I was so overwhelmed that I said … "I will write for free"

After a couple sports stories had been submitted, I realized that sports weren't my first love …. Being Black was, , I asked Bee could I just do editorials and she said sure , so over the years all I covered was editorials. So anything local or national that was having an effect on people of color I wrote about it. I went in hard and made it edgy on purpose. My dad was always worried cause I never held back, he was concerned for my safety but very proud at the same time showing my editorials to his poker buddies, I would always tell my dad, "whoever has a problem with my words then their the one with the problem, and plus Bee said it was cool"

Bee I just want to thank you from the bottom of my heart for accepting me as part of the

Urban Spectrum family, having my name listed as a writer always gave me chills. I remember dropping off my articles at the office , this was way before you could submit it through email and the staff there would ask "Dex what did you write about this month" they were waiting with anticipation cause they had an idea I had much shit to talk. You saw something in me I didn't know I had, for 30 years not once did you edit my words, you let it roll. You gave me the green light to be a "Prolific shit talker" ... Bee, thank you for many opportunities and for the love you have shown for 30 years. I would not be where I am with this writing stuff if not for you. I don't name drop but when I would tell people I know you and you're a good friend, they would be "wow you know her" that speaks volumes of the hard work you put in over the years, you're a legend, you're a mentor you're a boss and your my friend and we all love you.

Thanks so much, you made this dream of writing a book a reality, cause you saw something in me. You gave me that green light.

I love you Bee

Nikki

Thanks for coming into my life at the right moment, the right time.
Never thought our friendship would turn into something so wonderful so divine.
Even through hard times and crazy shit you had to endure.
You've been such a great Mom a career woman even an entrepreneur.
You been a solo artist never asking for help doing it on your own.
Because of your wonder kids, they made sure Mom's was never alone.
You always stayed true, stayed loyal, always there for me.
During our awkward times I knew I had you, I knew I had Nikki
You're that little dime piece, true Soul Sista, very Authentic Queen
I just had to say thank you, for being there always, you know what I mean.

Love You

Soul Sisters

These are two Christian sisters who take every step by Faith.
Never ever holding a grudge or showing signs of Hate
Their Spirit is so giving, a unique part of their Soul.
Always there for others, never letting you fall, ready to grab Hold.
I've always felt like family when asked over to their House.
Not once did I feel unwelcomed, even with my crazy Mouth.
No two can show love, quite like Bobbi & Lee
They've been there for my family, in every time of Need.
So full of Soul, many ways to look at it.
I'm their crazy big brother, don't ever get it Twisted.

Ms. Williams

My friend my bud the ultimate inspiration
It's our ride or die friendship based on dedication.
It's your stand tall never bend never break demeanor.
It's you never asking for help when you look it's just her.
It's your soul power, fist raised, yes that chick.
It's your proud black skin.... Original... very authentic
She's very proud. Very loyal a younger version of me
It's my ride or die best friend I simply call D.

Djuana

How can I begin to thank you, for all you've done to help me with my growth.

Never have I given a person with a nickname that has three letters," Ph.D" you're the first, you stand alone for who you are and what you represent. I know many people very important people, never have I Googled anyone, and they've taken up about six pages. That says a lot about your importance and contribution to many. But as I got to know you, your more than Dr. Harvell… much more.

I was able to have someone become a part of my life that cared so much for others and many times put others before herself. You have taken on many roles in trying to make a difference and the well-being of others. You sit on many committees to a fault at times, but you stayed focused and never stopped your drive and will power.

You're a woman of Christ who walks the walk every day and can somehow see the goodness in everyone that has crossed your path. Thank you for making sure my mental and emotions were always in a good place, you set the bar high for other young sista's to follow. Thank you for helping me become a better me and all the support in my many projects. A woman that's true to her family and her Delta Sisters (White Pearl Gang)
The daughter of Bobby & Sherri has done well.
If you need proof just Google her.
Thank you love you.